Ashen Leaves

Ashen Leaves

Barking Buddha Books

All rights reserved. No part of this publication may be reproduced, distributed, or transmitted in any form or by any means, including photocopying, recording, or other electronic or mechanical methods, without the prior written permission of the publisher, except in the case of brief quotations embodied in critical reviews and cetain other noncommercial uses permitted by copyright law. Printed in the United States of America.
Photo by Smeeta Mahanti Photography
ISBN #: 9798667408277

for Siddhartha Barack & Baba

ACKNOWLEDGMENTS

Writing these poems, for me, has been a special journey across time, place and people. There is no one in my life that I have met by chance or circumstance that hasn't left a mark in my life, however little or profound it might have been. In their life and death, everyone throughout my life has enabled me to become the person I am today. Our relationships have given rise to poetry that will forever remain etched in this book.

There are so many people to whom I owe a lot of gratitude. These are people whose love and blessings have carried me through the happiest and saddest moments in my life. I thank each of you from the bottom of my heart for all your support, love and kindness.

To my parents, Sandhya & Dilip – Thank you for all your sacrifices. I owe my life to you both. Baba, I wish you were here today. I miss you and you continue to live in me.

To my brother, Deepak – You have always been there for me. I am grateful for everything you have done for me. Love you from the bottom of my heart.

To my aunt and uncle Bharati & Kamalesh – Thank you for raising me and loving me like your own. Nothing I do or say will ever make up for what you have done for me.

To my cousins Mrinalini, Meenakshy, Mana & Anisha Our bonds are precious and I was fortunate to have shared so many wonderful times with you all through the years.

To my in-laws, Joyasree & Subhendra Dev – Thank you for your love, patience and understanding. I am truly blessed to have you both in my life.

To my sisters-in-law Kimberly Lynn & Smeeta – Thank you for showing me what it means to be sisters.

To my nannies, Maushi & Suman – You both cradled me from birth and cared for me through the years. You have taught me how to be humble, kind and selfless.

To all my family and friends who read my poetry and encouraged me to publish this book.

To all my mentors who continue to inspire and guide me.

To my Editor & Book Producer, Hiram Sims and his talented team – Princess Indigo & Sean Slaughter – for bringing this book to life.

To our son, Siddhartha Barack – Bringing you into this world has made me complete and taught me what it means to love something so dearly that it hurts. My love and blessings to you. O' Lil Boy. I love you with all of my heart and my soul.

To our Atom – With you kind eyes and gentle soul, you are more like my son than the Husky-Shepherd people see. Thank you for your unconditional love and companionship. Love!

To my husband, Sanjit – Thank you from every inch of my heart for your love, support and belief in me. Bringing Sid into this world with you has been the greatest gift ever. Here's to 06.06.06! Love you.

TABLE OF CONTENTS

- 14 The Left Behinds
- 15 Losing You
- 16 Grieving To Grieve
- 18 I Did Not Go Looking For Death
- 19 The End
- 21 Over
- 22 El Malecon
- 22 A Marriage
- 24 I Wish
- 25 I Thought Of You Today
- 26 O' Lil Boy
- 28 I Am
- 29 And There It Was
- 30 You Break My Heart
- 31 You Look At Me
- 32 Ashen Leaves
- 33 Light
- 34 Plucked
- 35 How Can I
- 36 With Each Passing Day
- 38 Odds And Ends
- 39 Painful
- 40 Your Arms
- 41 Roads
- 42 Fireflies
- 43 I Didn't Say Goodbye
- 45 Gentle Resistance
- 46 Almost Certain
- 47 Old Fashioned
- 48 Midnight Rendezvous
- 49 Will You Forgive
- 50 You

51	Side By Side
52	I See You
53	I Never Asked You
54	Sometimes
55	We Walked
56	Moments Pass
57	Closed Eyes
58	Around Your Casket
60	Sleep
61	Let This Night
62	Milk & Honey
63	Perhaps You Will
64	I Lost Your Face
65	I Cannot Think
67	I Walk Alone
68	In The Shadows
69	You've Harnessed Me
70	In Your Touch
71	Don't Be Lost
72	Let Me Never
73	My Eyes Wouldn't Close
74	My Heart Pains
75	The Moon
76	Am I Ready
77	Fill Me
78	I Do Not Want
79	I Want To Lay
80	Treasure Chest
81	You Seem To Be
82	Withdrawal
83	This World Is Cruel
84	I Feel My Body

TABLE OF CONTENTS

85	No Turning Back
86	My Heart Can
87	Your Body
88	I Like You
89	My Heart Awoke
90	Beautiful Remorse
91	Spring Blossom
92	It's Hard For Me To Breathe
93	I Sit Here
94	Today
95	Your Voice
96	Sorrow
97	In The Shadows
98	The Tango
99	The Night Is Upon Us
100	My Heart Cried For You Yesterday
101	Silent Tears Fall
102	Where Do Your Thoughts Go
103	Smoke In The Air
104	Inflamed
105	Just Like Flowers
106	Too Familiar
107	Weightless
108	Loving and Missing
109	What Draws You To Me
110	The Electricity Of Us
111	Until You
112	Tasty Pleasures
113	I Can Still Taste You
114	Lock and Key
115	Will It Be Wrong
116	Don't Be Fooled

117	Rejection
118	I've Stopped Making Sense
119	Downtown At 7:05
120	The Simpleness Of Us
121	Grief
122	Just Words
123	You Churned My Life
124	Snow Cones
125	Midnight
126	Mind & Heart
127	Where Did You Go
128	I Don't Think
129	Fire Burns
130	Searching For Me
131	It Is That Look You Give Me
132	Invisible
133	Just When Life
134	After A Long Time
135	Sway With Me
136	Ruth's Flight
137	Disillusioned
138	The Sky Is Falling
139	The Color Of My Skin
140	Space
141	Into My Soul
142	Tenderness
143	Will You Remember Me
144	In Secret

PREFACE

I find poetry to be much like people. Not every poem has to be liked by everyone. Not every poem will speak to everyone. As a poet, my hope is that each poem will find its home in the heart and mind of another besides my own.

Writing emotions and experiences in the form of verse is a form of art that I have admired since childhood. To be able to express in just a few words and cause profound feelings through them is something every poet wishes for. I have learned from many poets of the past and those in the present whose words have educated and inspired me. I would like to thank them all for giving me the courage to put my own words into print.

This collection has been many years in the making. The poems you will read in this book appear in no particular chronologic or thematic pattern. Just as life and emotions, they are random, and often times unpredictable. These poems are a collective of emotions, observations and expressions that are personal and universal to many of us.

Stay Well, Go Well.

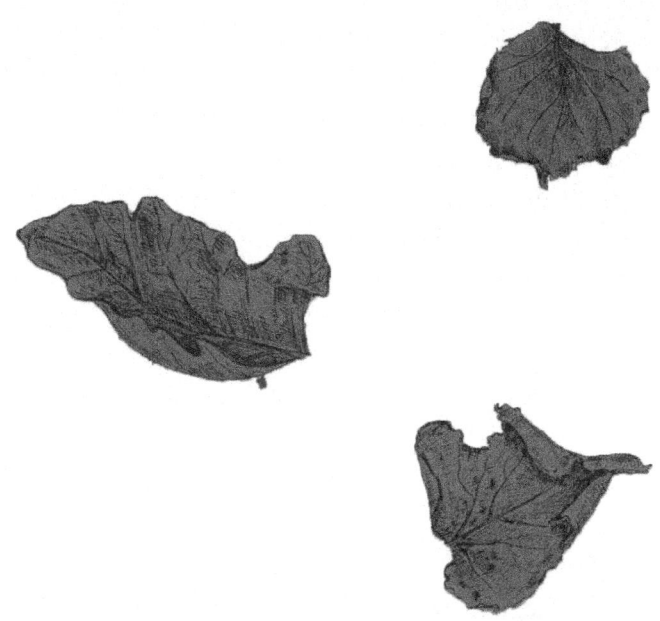

THE LEFT BEHINDS

We are the left behinds
Not the forgotten
Not the begotten
But the left behinds
What do they know
of the heartaches they cause
when they deliver and forget
then reclaim what they lost?
What do they know
of what this heart also feels?
The love you gave them
you can't reclaim when in need
To them we are
what we never had in mind
Not the forgotten
Not the begotten
But only the left behinds

LOSING YOU

I feel
I am losing you
to something
Why that is
I do not know
But its existence is
like air
Invisible in its form
but strong in its conviction
Pulling you away from me
in a tug of war
felt only by my aching heart

GRIEVING TO GRIEVE

A body, cold and heavy
What did he feel as he left this world behind?
Was he afraid? Was he in pain? Was he confused?
What was he thinking as he took those final breaths?
Was he ready? Was he prepared?
Did he lose faith, or did he just give up?
Questions and more questions.

Standing by this cold calm body I do not know how to feel
I cannot cry
I cannot think
Touching his body only makes me feel hollow
His eyes are closed
His face not entirely rested
I could just wake him
His hair looks gray and overgrown
I am upset he hasn't had a haircut
I remember sitting on the porch and trimming it for him
Did he want me to feel the guilt?
I want to take a scissor and trim it
again and again and again.

I took the same flight he took
I try to imagine where he sat
I try to imagine him with his scotch and soda
His body does not smell like him anymore
How many times I might have
wanted him to shower
to wash his sweat away
I miss it now.

I look around me
So many people here
I don't know who they are
They come up to me, nearly all of them
I cannot hear their words
I cannot think their thoughts
I want them all to leave me alone as he vanishes in flames
His ashes warm and gray do not comfort me.

This night is dark
Darker than ever before
I finally feel the emptiness
A candle illuminates his picture
It burns itself out as the sunlight hits my face.
For a decade now I have woken up each day and slept
every night searching for answers
Today, I will let go of him
Today, I will free myself
Today, I will grieve for us
Today, I will celebrate.

I DID NOT GO LOOKING FOR DEATH

I did not go looking for death
It was she who sought me
One warm afternoon
In my cold room
With barren walls
With tubes and all
It was she who came to me
I resisted a little at first
unannounced in her company
And although my voice could not be heard
amidst those lines and monitors
she wooed my soul to hers in perfect harmony
A feeling of liberation
Beautiful
Surreal
I had seen her many times before
Pushed her far away
But this time her presence so calm and warm
would take my heart away
She pulled me up
She pulled me out
until I saw me down there
My loved ones all gathered near
Unsure and unaware
I took my breath
I found my peace
In my mind I began to pray
My soul prepared as
This time I knew
my end was here to stay

THE END

The end
is near in sight
yet so far away
as my flesh breaks down each day
unable to support my body that showcases my bones

The end
is near in sight
yet so far away
so much pain
"Go on" they say
Another round of chemo
"You can't give up,
even though we know you are too weak."

The end
is near in sight
yet so far away
My hope keeps me afloat.
My little boy's eyes don't see what's to come
as he sits with his toy car on the hospital bed,
thinking I will come home this weekend
and read to him his favorite book.

The end
is near in sight
yet so far away
that my lips can't feel my lover's kiss anymore.
Our love is now ethereal.
My body numb all around,
unable to return his desire.

The end
is near in sight
yet so far away
that I keep fading
every second
of every minute
of every day
of every week
of every month
of every year
since the diagnosis
just waiting for
The End

OVER

Over
Sipping this red wine
I reflect on his words
It's over
life
marriage
emotions
expressions
As wine fills my veins
over and over and over

EL MALECON

Wall against water
stuck in time
of lovers and friends
seeking answers
beyond their minds
Of revolutions and war
into freedom of thought
escaping into the waves
that beat against this rock
Of writers and painters
and dances and song
this land is opportunity
oppressed and wronged
Wall against water
shielded from time
a nation left dreaming
beyond the tides

A MARRIAGE

A Marriage
is like a massage
It's all about
pressure & touch
Too hard
and it's sheer agony
Too light
and it's unsatisfying
The right pressure & touch
however
keeps you yearning
for more

I WISH

I wish
The roof above my head
was yours
The coffee in my hand
you could afford
The warm water my skin felt
you could drench in too
The chicken tenders my boy eats
you could taste
How cruel is life
How sad is my heart
I must wake up
from my entitlement

I THOUGHT OF YOU TODAY

I thought of you today
and perhaps you thought of me
as I read the passing away of another
whose words spoke to us in unity
This madness of silence created
is crippling and unclear
and like the person itself
these emotions
will disappear
I will not apologize
And neither should you
You've chosen the way a pendulum swings
in a favor or two
I want you to be happy
and it might just as well be that
if your happiness is through others
I shall let you free

O' LIL BOY

O' Lil Boy, O' Lil Boy
Who will you be
Will you be the one
that sits lonely under a tree?
Will you be the one
who dreams his troubles away?
Or will you be the one
whose dreams just fade away?
Will you be the one
who runs away in fear,
or will it be you who stands your ground
and helps those that are near?
Will you be the one
to give to those in need,
or will your life be destined to be a thief?
Will you be the one
who nurtures and protects
or will you be the one whose hands commit
something they regret?
Will your heart see through
the pain another has endured,
or will you be the one
who is responsible for their tears?
Whatever your fate may be,
remember O' Lil Boy
There was someone who held you close
and loved you when you cried
She sang to you and read you books
and gently put you to sleep
With a prayer each night
for your bright light
to shine a real good deed

So whatever you decide to be
O' Lil Boy
Remember me my dear,
my eyes will be watching you
And I pray not in fear.

I AM

I am
my father's hopes
my mother's dreams
my sister's aspirations
my own mystery
I am
the voice of justice
the heart of love
the tears of failure
the laughs of youth
I am
too comfortable with wheelchairs
too bothered with injustice
too young to think deep
too old to be weak
I am
a friend
a singer
a poet
a writer and more
Inside me hides a photographer
with a lens very clear
Alas,
all of this I am
That is for sure
but what I shall grow up to be
is still so unclear

AND THERE IT WAS

And there it was
That last breath
Profound yet serene in its exit
There was no conviction in it
Just a sad, solemn acceptance
of the impermanence
that was always meant to be
At the moment of her death,
she finally looked complete
Her lips still warm
A blue hue set over her skin
Much like Picasso
and his dead woman
A masterpiece in life
A masterpiece in death
Free at last

YOU BREAK MY HEART

You break my heart
by pushing me
to be better
than I am
To understand
the complex web
woven in life
that you have lived
and learned from
To not be shallow
but elevate every soul
that interjects
in my life
Whether by choice
or circumstance

YOU LOOK AT ME

You look at me
from across the room
Your eyes
speak too much
I cannot
return their gaze
I am afraid
they ask too much
We cannot be
one
I am not
strong enough
to overcome
the years of hate
I have
built up for you
Hoping that one day
you will come back
for me
And now you have
but
a little too late

I have moved on

ASHEN LEAVES

Ashen leaves
fall
on wicker chairs
and wooden planks
traveling from a distance
scorched by fire
they keep their shape
so delicate
in black and gray
floating
along with the wind
in directions
unknown to them

They have said their goodbye
They have left their home
They have lost their breath
Yet graceful
in their charred form
they land on my palm
only to be blown away
into dust

LIGHT

Light
This weight
off my finger
Now bare
the tan
slowly receding

Light
A weight
off my finger
Heavy heart
Heavy tears
Heavy hurt
Heavy fears

So light that
it feels so heavy
A heaviness
I don't like
Anymore

PLUCKED

Plucked
underneath you
I crave the pain
I feel inside me
along with the tenderness
your lips
bestow on mine
to remind me
of the harmony
that is us

HOW CAN I

How can I
make a change?
So many thoughts
crowd my head
I'm overwhelmed
for me, for you, for us
No decision will ever be
too wrong or right
No choice will ever be
too hard or easy
We stand here
in between
life and death
heaven and earth
happiness and sorrow
lost and found
Each one of us
in this moment
of inexplicable
belonging and not
moving forward
with every second
in only one direction
of inevitable
ultimate
impermanence

WITH EACH PASSING DAY

With each passing day
For some of us
it is true
Things get confusing
and complicated
and we don't know
what to do
Situations unforeseen
come to you
one by one
and all they do is
tie you in a knot
Is there a way out?
A narrow escape?
Who knows
the right answers
Who knows
what will stay
A glimmer of hope perhaps?
Or a cloud
with a silver line
I don't know where to start
It is convoluting my mind
I reach out to you
There are no regrets, per se
because the hole
you dragged me into
seems so close
to yesterday
The years

are passing on
My heart
is beyond light
I shall move on again today
into this dark cold night

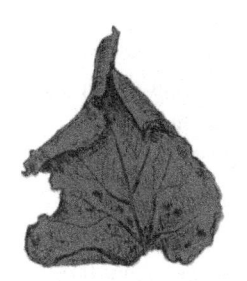

ODDS AND ENDS

Odds and Ends
of many things
lay scattered on the floor
Amidst all of them
a photograph of yours
Toys
Books
Clothes
Diapers and much more
A bottle
A blanket
all sit across the floor
The empty suitcase stands upright
against the barren walls
The closet filled with silence
with nothing in it at all
The life this room had cradled once
The laughter and the tears
The coos and babbles
that filled each passing ear
The stroller and the sun
The crib that stood in the room
With all of that our imaginations vanished
With a pacifier or two
Gone are the years
we dreamed of once
with you as forever and more
And now the pain is too real
we can no longer seem to endure

PAINFUL

Painful
as it may be
we need to part
The years will
simply
wash away the tears
and time will
erase
the memory of us
only to emerge
as distant reminders
of what was then
and what could have been

YOUR ARMS

Your arms
surround
me whole
and keep
me warm
holding
my breasts
in gentle
caress
to protect
me from
my own
insecurity
that pulls
at me
from
inside out

ROADS

As she curves
amidst
the mountains
she awakens me
in seduction
carrying me
to a place
I've only dreamed of
feeling my legs
quiver
as the lingering
continues
Naked
as the valley
welcomes us
underneath
the blanket of blue
that shields my flower
as life
reveals
its desires

FIREFLIES

Fireflies
shimmer across this field
as I think of you
with a warm glow
in my heart
The days we sat
for hours at a time
when you taught me
the meaning of life
I think of those days now
sitting
with little hands in my palm
watching these fireflies
light up the darkness
singing songs
we once sang
together
hoping that one day
he too will
gaze at these wonders
and keep the memories
alive

I DIDN'T SAY GOODBYE

I didn't say goodbye
to you this morning
Still upset that
you came home
late last night
past your curfew
Still mad that you
didn't clean your room
or wash your dinner plate
I hoped you'd say good morning
as you took your pop tart
and stormed out the door
Still upset at me
from the night before
I didn't imagine
that I wouldn't see you
ever again
or see you walk
through the door
That I would never
kiss you goodnight
or get to see you
blossom and grow
I wish I had
said goodbye to you
I wish I had
held you some more

I'm sorry
I was wrong
It's too late now
I know
They told me
you are already
at heaven's door

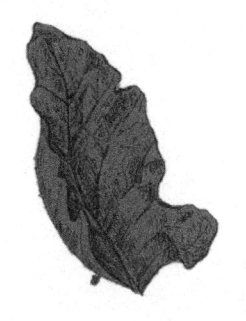

GENTLE RESISTANCE

Push and pull
this
tug of war
between
the breaths
that
wait to fade
into cinder
one
with earth
the gentle resistance
of impermanence

ALMOST CERTAIN

Almost certain
that my heart races
as I see you
amidst the crowds
and just like that
in those moments
I wonder why
I need to reckon
as one force
with you
in protective insecurity
that fades with time
as my eyes connect
to meet your smile
into a world
safe and secure
amidst the chaos
that surrounds us

OLD FASHIONED

Dusky Orange
of whiskey or rye
The swirl of liquor
tempting the eyes
Through the glass
heaviness resides
Sipping slowly
as thoughts unwind
The taste
The times
The men
The crimes
As memories awake
of moments in space
Sweetness and bitter
seduction create

MIDNIGHT RENDEZVOUS

Midnight rendezvous
of distant tides
Precious moments
the meeting of minds
Awake and aware
awaiting time
To feel that magic
magnetic and blind
Of words and verses
and thoughts and more
Of human bonds
on distant shores
Bodies heavy
hearts too light
A state of dreams
that wraps us tight
The hours now
feel long and drawn
My eyes onlooking
a saffron dawn
that ends the night
in pure delight
as I lay down
and close my eyes

WILL YOU FORGIVE

Will you forgive
all my imperfect emotions
as you try to understand
my foolishness
whilst I too try to understand
where and why through life
we wander to find exactly
what we need
but cannot
have

YOU

You
Taught me to cook
Helped me clean
Gave me hope
Encouraged my dreams
Understood my fears
Suppressed my beasts
Consoled my tears
Held me through grief
The cracks we now face
are extremely severe
The noise it creates
is difficult to hear
The pain it causes
is difficult to bear
Sometimes it feels
we just don't seem to care
Just know that
since we parted
never a moment
is spared
without you
in my heart
for you are
and always
forever there

SIDE BY SIDE

I felt your hand
brush
against my back
and I could tell
it was not by
chance
I didn't turn around
and you didn't
despair
Our hearts understood
what our minds
couldn't dare
I watched you
all night
through the corner
of my eyes
avoiding your gaze
every moment
you smiled
And then
just like that
as I walked
into the night
I found you
waiting for me
and we walked
side by side

I SEE YOU

I see you
lying gently
on the bed
breathing
so light
that feathers
might not
take flight
And
in your face
I find
an invitation
to feel
your lips
against mine
soft as ever
as you gently
allow me
to taste you
inside out
caressed
in your arms
as I gaze
into
your eyes

I NEVER ASKED YOU

I never asked you
why
we couldn't be
after the years we spent
lying down
in each other's arms
through pain and pleasure
day or night
as raindrops splashed
on the window
while crackling wood
often with its glow
awoke us
our legs intertwined
so often
as the winters cold subsided
with your skin
naked and warm
against mine
draped in sheets
on the bed
that we both picked
longingly
years ago
thinking
nothing would
change

SOMETIMES

Sometimes
it is
easier
just to
let go
the love
a heart feels
when
the connection
is so strong
that
It defeats
even
beautiful things
along the way

WE WALKED

We walked
through the gardens
side by side
silently
hand in hand
as we reminisced
the pain and love
of years long lost
in moments left behind
We stopped
on the bridge
over the pond
and stood
to see the koi
colored in shades
of orange and black
waving their curvy tails
towards us
unaware
that we too
at one time
waded
in each other's arms
only to be lost
to each other
with time

MOMENTS PASS

Moments pass
across
mountains and tides
The night gives in
to morning rise
Flowers awake
with dewdrops atop
The grass still wet
from melting frost
A curtain of warmth
covers the fields
The river glistens
into gentle streams
The birds still glide
across the sky
In patterns mesmerizing
to every eye
If only these moments
we stopped to see
To breathe the air
of uncertainty
I feel for me
my heart would know
When to stop
and say no more

CLOSED EYES

As pain
consumed
my eyes
from light
I closed them
gently
only to find
a curtain
of darkness
illuminating
my inner thoughts
and guiding me
to infinite
clarity

AROUND YOUR CASKET

Around your casket
as people stand in black
and wail
from grief
I stand aside
and rejoice
your freedom
from this life

To others
it seems like
I am the ungrateful one
who had spent years
by your side
now to appear so apathetic
as we all gathered
to give you a farewell
on their terms

Their grief
so momentary
is loud and harsh
We both know
their tears will dry
as your casket drops
into the earth
covered with flowers
and holy dirt

It is only natural
they all will retire
to their lives
and soon to them
you will be
just a memory

For me of course
I shall sit
alone in our home
by our bay window
sipping my tea
mixed with tears
alone

In your absence
rewinding
my thoughts
on our life
together
in sickness and health
in good times and bad
remembering
that we
only had each other
until death
really did
do us apart

SLEEP

Sleep
last night
was a tender
moment
in time
as my body
gave in
to the paintings
etched
in my mind
seducing
us both
to a hopeless
yearning
surreal
with colors
that slowly
exploded in
my heart

LET THIS NIGHT

Let this night
seduce you
to a space
deep inside
your most secret
desires
so that you
awaken tomorrow
feeling
nothing is
lost

MILK & HONEY

To me
you taste
like
Milk & Honey
rationed
in desperate times
Sleepy sweetness
just enough
to satisfy
a craving
that needs
to stay calm
until
the tide
comes in
again

PERHAPS YOU WILL

Perhaps you will
always love me
the way you have
from the moment we
kissed
on the stairwell
curved in iron

When youth
was in our bodies
perfected
by the clothes we wore
that fell to the ground
as we made love
across the world
in space and time

As our bodies moved
in satin sheets
with divine pleasures
only lovers can feel
insatiable
to each other

I LOST YOUR FACE

I lost your face
as music
filled my ears
and
intoxicated my mind
with secret thoughts
unknown to you
as
you pulled me
gently
into your arms
lost
in your own thoughts
unknown to me
as our bodies
danced
to their own tune
evoking a magic
that brought us
back
to each other
in
reckless abandon

I CANNOT THINK

I cannot think
of losing you
in the midst
of this chaos
that has consumed
each one of us
giving rise to
many unknowns
As we see
even the strong ones
crumble and give in
to something
far from what
our minds dared
to imagine
As these dark times
swiftly sweep away
our loved ones
and fear builds
in small doses
on this earth
reminding us
of the preciousness
of each breath
taken too lightly
by each one of us
I know that if
there was to be
a sacrificial alter
I would offer myself
so that you

may live to see
another day
towards
redemption

I WALK ALONE

I walk alone
on these empty streets
Where once
in recent times
I might have waited a while
to cross the intersection
There's now only
another couple in sight
across the road
with masks covering
their smiles
as they walk
in haste
The beauty of this city
is more apparent now
in its barren despair
of the times
As the mountains
stand bold
and trees
appear tender green
after the rains
Their presence
almost stark
in the emptiness
that surrounds this
City of Angels
that seems
so lost
in time

IN THE SHADOWS

In the shadows
of the unknown
we walk somber
against time
The clock ticking
in infinite beat
only to itself
as we wait
our turns
for kismet
to roll the dice
maintaining
our poker faces
in the anguish
of our times

YOU'VE HARNESSED ME

You've harnessed me
amidst the storm
that circled around me
for hours yesterday

And just like that

I've settled down
tamed by
nothing more
than just your
silence

IN YOUR TOUCH

In your touch
there's a magic
that makes me
come alive
soft and gentle

I want the feeling
to last forever
as I move
to the music
you create
in me

DON'T BE LOST

Don't be lost
to me
amidst the silence
I want to
hear you
breathing
the sultry air
as lust
unfolds
my petals
under
your skin

LET ME NEVER

Let me never
lose my mystery
in your eyes
as you uncover me
in your desire
Let me walk
into your arms
and be able
to walk out
of them
even more
mysterious
to you

MY EYES WOULDN'T CLOSE

My eyes wouldn't close
for hours last night
Thinking of you
I travelled
across many lines
I lay in bed restless
as time passed on by
with sensations
stronger
than words can describe
And when it was done
my mind was clear
from guilt and norms
and societal fears
For in waking today
with a clearer mind
I could feel a calm
that won't subside
I feel ready
as much as can be
to walk this path
in ecstasy

MY HEART PAINS

My heart pains
with the thought
that that I might
have hurt yours
My body is tired
restless in bed
unable to sleep
thinking of why
I feel you should
know my every thought
and feelings around
people and words
of yesterday
when I know
you are above
it all

THE MOON

The moon
is hidden tonight
amidst the clouds
for fear that
it shall light up
my eyes
through which
you could see
my deepest desires
that remain buried
inside my heart
tearing me apart
as I slowly
recede
when I see you walk
towards me
waiting to
unfold the passion
that cripples me

AM I READY

Am I ready
for you
to see
all my imperfections
all the scars
and changes
life has imprinted
on my youth

Am I ready
for you
to discover
my deepest wounds
and softest curves
that evoke the passion
that waits to be
devoured
by your touch

Am I ready
for you
to take me to a place
from which returning
to today
will be beyond
impossible

Am I ready

FILL ME

Fill me
with your eternal love
in ways
that I may feel you
in my loins
in every waking moment
causing a revolution
underneath my soft
chocolate skin
that flows like
a sweet fondue
on your tongue

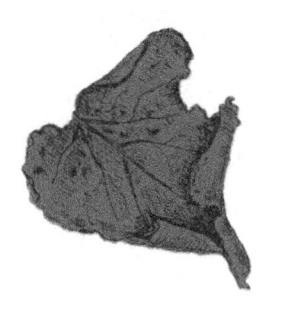

I DO NOT WANT

I do not want
to die alone
without a single soul
by my side
I want to feel
the touch
of another
I want my thoughts
to subside
in the darkness
my mind feels
as my heart
sits still in
this loneliness
with my body
waiting by this
glass
that stands between
life and death

I WANT TO LAY

I want to lay
wrapped up in your arms
in silence
so that the only sound
I hear is
the breaths we take
I feel I could lay there
forever
in wakeful sleep
on hot afternoons
or cold winter nights
as hours turn to days
that flow into weeks
which blossom into years
towards eternity
I want to lay
wrapped up in your arms
until you decide
it's time

TREASURE CHEST

My mind
is like a
treasure chest
buried
under the seas
with secrets
and pleasures
only for
you and me

YOU SEEM TO BE

You seem to be
the only one
who can seal
this feeling
of my incompleteness
through life
as I wander
through it aimlessly
without a purpose
or a mission
looking for
meaning
to harness
this lost soul

WITHDRAWAL

Withdrawal from you
is worse than liquor
I can get that
whenever I want
from the wooden bar
in my living room
Withdrawal from you
is worse than opioids
Those I can stop
once the pain subsides
as flesh seals
and scars appear
Withdrawal from you
is worse than coffee
Tea and Tylenol can
cure that in no time
Withdrawal from you
is gloomy
sucking me hollow
with no antidote in sight

THIS WORLD IS CRUEL

This world is cruel
so hold me close
I feel a sense of
loneliness taking over
and I want to be
in the arms of love
holding me near
a beating heart
as I cry my fears
and sob my pains
as sadness consoles grief
and sleep takes over
as I find shelter
in the warmth
of your arms

I FEEL MY BODY

I feel my body
moving along with
yours into a divine
space where the
only thing I feel
is the quivering of
my lips as you
evoke my womanhood
with your bare hands
And then
as your lips touch mine
I feel you
deep within my
soul as your eyes
pull me into theirs
into a different
universe

NO TURNING BACK

There's no turning
back
from where we've been
today
I return to that place
often
in my mind with closed
eyes
that can see us as
one
against all tides
lost
in each other as if
this
was how it was
meant
to always be

MY HEART CAN

My heart can
see yours
as you silently wait
and try to make sense
of today
My heart can
feel the pain
you feel as the
rains come down
and dampen the earth
as you seek rays
of hope in the sky
My heart can hear
you calling
as you yearn
with your body and soul
nothing more than a tenderness
within the dry walls painted in white
My heart can tell
when you've given in
to the distance
you didn't create
along the years as life drifted along
My heart can tell
when it needs to beat with yours
when your voice echoes
in my ears from afar
reaching out to mine

My heart can tell

YOUR BODY

Your body
sucks me in
exploring each
inch and ounce
of my flesh
lying next to you
naked
as we embrace
for a moment
in a different
universe
where nothing
is forbidden
in infinite passion
as our warm bodies
intertwine
and give in
to our deepest
desires

I LIKE YOU

I like you
because you are different
from my day to day
In you
I can escape
into a world more
soft and serene
unphased
by any force that
pulls me apart
in different
directions

MY HEART AWOKE

My heart awoke
crying this morning
facing the gloomy
dawn unlike the usual
sunny blue skies
that cover this city

Right now there is
a coldness that
shatters us all
keeping even lovers apart
as longing and desire
consume the mind
and dusk
slowly lends
to empty nights

BEAUTIFUL REMORSE

I don't feel
beautiful in my skin today
For scars from a time
long before you
depress my mind

When the sheer innocence
of my childhood
was destroyed
in just one stroke
that hurt like
daggers from inside out

I have tried to recall
how those moments
forced me
into womanhood
overnight
in my little skin
still blossoming
amidst the pain

SPRING BLOSSOM

Silent through the winter
she blossoms in spring
Her tender leaves
filling up the naked brown
in a cloak of green
with yellow hues
looking up at the sun
and inviting the rays
to shine through her
as if to say
I'm ready for you
from the days last year
where I left
my other self to become
who you see me today

IT'S HARD FOR ME TO BREATHE

It's hard for me to breathe
I cannot begin to explain
this feeling building up
in my chest
of heaviness in my breasts
as I think of you talking them softly
between your lips and teasing them
as I move to your music

With your touch I feel
a desire to be desired
and a seduction so pure
that my breath softly ceases
as the seconds pass on by
with you exploring my curves
and imperfections imprinted by life

And as you find your way
to become one with me
the rains begin to fall
and wetness wipes away
all my fears
all at once
and I am yours

I SIT HERE

I sit here
thinking of what you
may or may not be doing
right now in your home
I wonder if you have
a favorite chair
or drink
that you retire to
as you bask
in the beauty of
of the future
and the roots you planted
with love and tenderness
I wonder in those times
if you think of me
if I cross your mind
even for a fleeting second
and if I even fit in your world
of perfect
imperfections

TODAY

Today
I put you aside
and I did what most do
when missing someone
so much that nothing
in reality seems to be the way it should be
I did all my chores
and I read the paper
Then I took a long walk
and took in some fresh air
to come back home
to everyone and everything that waited
I did this all because I woke up today
missing you more than the other days
I don't know why
but today your absence
pained my heart
and threw me into a space
that was crippling
to my very soul

YOUR VOICE

Your voice
pierces
through my skin
slicing my flesh
splitting my organs
crushing my bones
And after it has done all that
it continues
to pierce through my veins
and mix in with my blood
that explodes through
every hole in my body
killing my spirit
and my soul
with your words

SORROW

Suddenly I feel
the sorrow building
in my heart
as I think of us
knowing that we
are so perfect together
when we touch
in those moments
that are so few
so sacred and scarce
to both of us
as we escape
the imperfections
that have been created
by life

IN THE SHADOWS

I can't seem to walk
in the shadows too well
I feel a subtle oppression
from the darkness that covers me
like an invisible cloak to everyone
And everything that seems alive
is beyond my grasp
as the pull from inside
keeps me from breaking out
of this cocoon we have woven

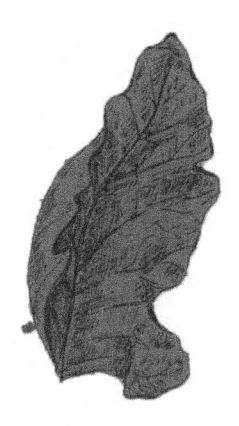

THE TANGO

We become
moments in time
as life and death
dance together
in a tango
hand in hand
feet so swift
their bodies touching
too close at times
that they appear one
as they blur the boundaries
between them
pushing and pulling
each other
into their universe
as we stand by
to watch
which of them
takes the prize

THE NIGHT IS UPON US

The night is upon us
with its moonlit sky
and tiny sparkles so beautiful
that they hide the ugly truth
we have been living
as the unknown continues
on this diseased earth
bodies burn far and wide
in so many directions that even
the compass of life
cannot keep steady
in this wake of those
who have left us
and the smell of death lingers
as the moon shines through
each crossing cloud
untouched by all
glorious each minute
looking down on us
as we narrowly escape our turn
to join those that went
before us

MY HEART CRIED FOR YOU YESTERDAY

My heart cried for you yesterday
and then tears began to flow
as I lay in bed
for all I could see
were your eyes
looking into mine
and all I could think of is why
we were destined to be
now more than before
even if not for eternity

And now my heart aches again
with pain you have endured
what if this is a mistake
what if destiny was somehow forced
what if our love is too sacred
that nothing will compromise
Is our love the reason this heart needs
to find its own demise

SILENT TEARS FALL

Silent tears fall
No one can see
No one can hear
this solemn misery
No one knows
how deep sits this pain
No one knows if
it will be dulled by the rains
Nobody can feel
the anger inside
No one can know
what secrets we hide
No one should care
what happens in time
No one will know
the love we sacrifice
And now
silently the knife
cuts deeper everyday
The pain and the glory
forever here to stay

WHERE DO YOUR THOUGHTS GO

Where do your thoughts go
as you feel the water touch your skin
Do you think of the days you cannot get back
or the hurt you cannot fix
as you swim weightless in your space
Do you feel the very weight of time
pushing you down a current only you can see
endless and with crimes
as you search your heart to find answers
to a life that could be free
Do you hear your splashing amongst the voices
that slowly drive you to insanity

SMOKE IN THE AIR

Smoke in the air
of circles and streams
My mind is high
with irreplaceable scenes
That lusty touch
with a glass of wine
Seductive moments
with legs entwined
Skin so warm
naked and soft
Kisses that taste
like chocolate drops
Smoke in the air
of circles and streams
I'm entering a land
of magical dreams

INFLAMED

Suddenly appear
the chills in my bones
All through the spine
from my chest to my toes
And unlike before
It's unbearable this time
There isn't a good reason
There isn't a rhyme
These moments that pass
are difficult to bear
I cannot sit still
Nothing compares
Breaths that I take
are far and few in between
Each feels like dagger
Each one is foreseen
My mind is distressed
My heart feels the pain
The insanity of this
is difficult to explain

JUST LIKE FLOWERS

Just like flowers
closing petals in the dark
from this world
I too shut my door
I too hide in the darkness
from demons and foes
to lay low on the ground
safe and secure

As light reappears
my fear disappears
and my petals begin to move
like flowers awaiting light
And as they open up with
the new dawn rising
my heart too begins to sing
with their calling

TOO FAMILIAR

I may have
become too familiar
to you that I sometimes fear
there no longer remains
the thrill you once
had for me
In waking moments
and moonlit nights
perhaps the reality
is too close and wronged
to keep this passion
amidst the wrath
that you don't need
and certainly don't deserve
as you conquer me and this universe

WEIGHTLESS

Weightless
with your beautiful body
you let the water wash your mind
clean of the fears and turmoils you
have seen today in your mind
Weightless
your mind travels slowly across the skies
to people and memories
in another place and time
Weightless
you let the voices around you
drown without a care
Your heart is in another world
you know that you won't share
Weightless
you sail a while
on the wide-open seas
until you're back to reality
and weight is all you feel

LOVING AND MISSING

Is there an art
to loving someone
without missing them
all the while

If there is
I want to know because
I can't seem
to figure it out

This love is consuming me
from inside out
and I have the feeling
of subliminal intoxication

WHAT DRAWS YOU TO ME

What draws you to me
is a mystery
You who are above so much
with all the beautiful seeds you've laid
What is it that draws you to this ordinary me
I don't get it
I don't understand it
And I'm confused as hell why you'd even
think to waste your time on someone like me
who compares nothing to the brilliance that
surrounds you at home and in life
And tears begin to fall
because I can't comprehend
why my heart found yours

THE ELECTRICITY OF US

The electricity of us
cannot be harnessed by wires
It cannot be touched by souls
and the holy trinity
It will not hide from demons
looking to suck out the nectar
Or those on earth
who weigh it down
The electricity of us
cannot be quenched by simple thirst
It needs water holier than in the holy grail
It will not give in to the reason
that cuts the current that runs through
our veins in unity creating
an energy so magnetic
that we become
unseen
unheard
unfelt
to all except
us

UNTIL YOU

Until you
I never understood what it meant
to want someone you can't have
Until you
I never understood
being born outside your time
Until you
I never understood
that it wouldn't matter at all
even if you could not love me
with all of your body
I would still love you fiercely
because my love for you
runs deep down in my marrow
Until you
I thought life went on
in one direction
with a sense of incomplete
Until you

TASTY PLEASURES

Like linguine soaking
up silken broth
Like single malt
in clanking glass
Like mussels soaked
in fine white wine
And blue cheese running
in honey sublime
Like caviar on
a bed of ice
And sea urchins in
their shells with spines
Like tequila
paired with perfect lime
Or brandied cherries
on a flambé pie
Like foie gras seared
with the sweetest grapes
Or falafel on a hummus plate
Like saffron strands in a biryani
I taste you almost incessantly

I CAN STILL TASTE YOU

I can still taste you
from that time
when you took my face
in your hands
and put your lips on mine
I can still feel the weight
of my body in your arms
As you pulled me down close
till our hearts beat as one
We lay naked under sheets
for moments not long
Every movement a treat
Every second a song
I can see you still sleeping
on the soft feather bed
My hand in your hand
My head in your chest
As days pass along
I carry these images with me
tucked deep in my heart
from our reality

LOCK AND KEY

I felt you knock
on my door
I saw you wait outside
It was about time I thought
for you to come inside
So one fine day
I left you a key
which took some time to find
You searched I know
high and low
frustrated like a child
Now you know
It was always there
Inside the flower pot
Its hidden glow
from head to toe
never meant to be sought
You picked it gently
as you should
and waited for a while
to welcome dusk
in all its lust
And all that it invites
I felt the key
slip in the lock
It held there for a while
And when you felt the raindrops fall
you gently slid inside

WILL IT BE WRONG

Will it be wrong
to imagine a life with you
although it can never be
Could I for a moment
be yours till I die
Without holy sanctimony
can we in our dreams
walk through the park
as lovers without no cares
Can we stand in the rain
or hop on a train
Can I imagine you
whisk me in air
Will it be wrong
if in my mind
we were meant to be
even though
we are now lost to each other
in our reality

DON'T BE FOOLED

Don't be fooled she said
You have to earn each prize
There's nothing that comes
free of anything
so learn to swallow that pride
Don't be fooled she said
You will always walk alone
There are those that are beside you
but never for too long
Don't be fooled she said
Guard your heart very tight
There will be pain along the journey
There will be regrets and despise
Don't be fooled she said
You've come a long way from before
Just walk as you have
until you can't walk no more

REJECTION

My heart felt
a piercing
that I didn't want to accept
However
I must learn to appreciate
the little gratuities
that come my way
insignificantly significant

I'VE STOPPED MAKING SENSE

I've stopped making sense
of everything that troubles me
The uncertainty of tomorrow
is a heaviness enough
that it pushes me
on the ground
against my own resistance
It questions my mind
for reason
and weighs on my emotions
for rationale
It makes me wonder
if I'm justified
when my desire
for you overpowers
all else that matters

DOWNTOWN AT 7:05

We met
downtown at 7:05
Both not knowing
what to expect
You took me by surprise
as you pulled me close
unsure even of yourself
That day
and in those hours
as uncertain as the times
I talked to you
about life and love
differently
than to any others before
And as you listened
I saw your eyes question
a deeper want
And I realized
You knew where I had been
You know where I am
And you wanted to go ahead
together

THE SIMPLENESS OF US

The simpleness of us
is something I wouldn't give up for
anything or anyone
To have moments in your arms
where the feeling of not a care in this world
feels eternal and right
To feel that love is all there is
and nothing other than we matter
for that time in space
and that the clock in life
has paused just for us
The simpleness of us is something
I wouldn't want to create again with
anyone else but you
For to suddenly wake up with the reality
that everything must end
makes it a reality too painful
to swallow

GRIEF

Grief
You came to me with your anticipation
Not surprised that I was blind
too sucked inside the tide
to realize I couldn't swim against time
You visited often in many forms
of emotions that went ignored
The chaos that surrounded me then
was something you would have cured
The promised hope of a life to save
didn't let me reason with you at all
Despite this you stayed with me
and watched me as I crawled
Like a loyal friend you reminded me
that I needed to let go
But by the time I turned to you
darkness had swallowed me whole

JUST WORDS

Why do I miss you so/she asked
Because you feel love/said he
Why do I love you so/she asked
You feel the adoration/said he

YOU HAVE CHURNED MY LIFE

You have churned my life
to create a butter so smooth
and delicious that
if I was a piece of burnt toast
the char would dissipate
as the silkiness on it
seeps through the grain
and reaches my tongue
the sweetness transforming
me into something
worthy of the gods

SNOW CONES

I like watching you
eat snow cones
with your tiny hands
Your favorite colors
making a rainbow
on the cold white ice
You slurp the liquid
with your favorite blue straw
with a smile that
speaks a thousand words
Your eyes a sparkling revelation
of your joy
in the simple delights
that every child should feel

MIDNIGHT

Midnight

and this city has slowed its tempo
from the beat of the day
I lie on my bed unable to move
from the heaviness I feel
from the weight of everything

Now and then as seconds move forward
my mind settles itself on a time from yesterday
thinking of the pain that runs through my bones settling
down where it wants to
sans explanation even to me

But then there is the memory of
soft lips I feel on my breasts
lips as delicate as peonies
and the touch of soft hands
hands so soft
that they take my womanhood
in their palms to open me up
like a flower waiting to bloom
so sensual and so enchanting that
even darkness cannot hide her smile
from our secrets

Midnight

MIND & HEART

Let go/says the mind
Hold on/says the heart
Run far/says the mind
Stay close/says the heart
It's complicated/says the mind
Keep it simple/says the heart
Stay strong/says the mind
Cry it out/says the heart
End it/says the mind
It's forever/says the heart

WHERE DID YOU GO

Where did you go
I can't find you anymore
I look for you everywhere
Traces of you remain
in every corner of my life
You have no idea how much
I've tried to put the pieces together
And the puzzle remains still unfinished
with shapes that do not fit anymore
I find myself looking
into the crowds and searching for you
although I know you are lost
Secretly hoping you too
are out there looking for me
And like a fairytale
we turn around to find
our eyes looking into each other

I DON'T THINK

In don't think
you spend any hours
in tears as I do
late at night
lamenting your love
I don't think
that even in a given moment
the existence of me
crosses the boundaries
or the thoughts you have
in your mind
interrupting your perfect life
that breaks you apart
enough to bring you
to your feet
when your reach out
to me in those bursts
that seem to last you forever
But they aren't good enough
to kill my tears
as I wait
missing you

FIRE BURNS

Fire burns
in this heart
Its flames invisible
to most all
Emotions charred
Collect into a pile of dust
and float away
from inside my mind
to some place outside
in space
to find their own place

SEARCHING FOR ME

There's a strange feeling
inside me that
subdues all else
as I look at the years gone by
where mediocrity at its best
is what I have to show for
nothing more nothing less
This feeling is so strong that it blurs
even the beautiful creations
I have brought into life
as if I have no worth
even to myself
constantly looking for something
unavailable and unreachable
like a sailboat lost at sea
searching desperately
for that lighthouse
on a distant shore

IT IS THAT LOOK YOU GIVE ME

It is that look you give me
in those moments
when you smile
uninhibited
and your eyes sparkle
along with your lips so
wet and irresistible
that seek an invitation
as they curve up
in an impish grin that
is so charming that
I can almost taste your
desire from afar

INVISIBLE

Invisible
we go on unseen
essential like air
needed in life
we fuel each other
Colorless
are the feelings
between you and me
hidden safely from all
in a magical world
undiscovered
Invisible and colorless
we walk together and apart
holding on to what we can
and letting go of all else

JUST WHEN LIFE

Just when life
happened to move
at its own pace
you came into it
and showed me what I was missing
and how everything I assumed
to be right was wrong
and that I deserved more
in life and in love
All this you showed me
as you shattered my present
with your perfection
leaving me lost
in my own reality

AFTER A LONG TIME

After a long time
I woke up and slid into your arms
to find that familiar place
from which I was slipping out
into a space that was foreign and insecure

As you pulled me closer and held me tight
I felt the warmth of your skin
and I knew life was going to be alright
and that we could just melt into
each other as we used to before

SWAY WITH ME

Sway with me
in winds that blow
across riverbeds
and mossy greens

Let's glide together
on frozen lakes
arm in arm
along the streams

Run with me
across the fields
hidden beneath
the bluest skies

Come my darling
walk with me
so I may never
leave your side

RUTH'S FLIGHT

Soft as the summer breeze
your breaths now
slow and steady
wait for their moment
to float away into the sky
and land on a cloud that
waits for you like a chariot
ornate and dressed
to take you to that place
sacred and special
with the grand procession
you deserve
in life and death
surrounded by angels
where you shall take
your throne beside
the other beautiful ones
that await your arrival

DISILLUSIONED

Disillusioned
by how people make decisions
in all aspects of life
Nothing seems to matter
when unfairness is the norm
and hard work and ethics
fall to the side
noticed but not enough
to be recognized
compared to the mediocrity
that continues to prevail

THE SKY IS FALLING

The sky is falling
No one to blame
The sun no longer
burns in flames
The stars are dim
The moon is quiet
No longer needing to guide the night
The heavens above look down below
to see on earth an angels glow
The rivers are flowing with silent tears
to fill the desert drought from years
My heart is hurting
in sorrow and despair
to think of today
and the news it bears

THE COLOR OF MY SKIN

The color of my skin
should not be why you
pin me down to my death
waiting patiently
with your hands
in your pocket
as mine are cuffed and
the air is sucked out of my body
from your idea of justice
The color of your skin
should not be the reason
you should have the right
to feel your worth is
more than mine
Because it isn't
We both came into this world
taking that breath that bore us life
And you don't get to play immortal

SPACE

You have to learn
to give people space
when you cannot
deal with your own anger
When your frustrations
build up enough
that you choose to
destroy others around you

I feel suffocated by
your arrogance that
assumes you are better
than all of us
in an entitlement that makes
me wonder why I should
give my heart to you
at all

INTO MY SOUL

Each time your eyes
look at me
I feel you are looking
into my soul
and you've wandered
into the deepest part of me
to find yourself reading
all the stories I have
sheltered from being
discovered

TENDERNESS

I need some tenderness today
I need a familiar touch
I need to hear a soothing melody
And quench this thirst for lust
I want to break away from rules
and feel free of all my ties
I want to walk this land liberated
Until the day I die

WILL YOU REMEMBER ME

Will you remember me, my love
when I am long gone
Will you remember
me waking up with you in the dawn
Will you remember my voice
and the songs I would sing
Will you remember my face
Resting soft on your skin
Will you remember my hands
holding yours in the night
Will you remember my lips
as we kissed in moonlight
Will you remember these moments
through the years of our past
Will you remember me, my love
so we may never part

IN SECRET

In secret our eyes speak
of desires we know
Sacred are our moments
wherever we go
Promised feelings of unending ties
to stand together side by side
These fleeting moments like a tide
bring in a surf that cannot subside
Words unspoken with eyes open wide
You and me shall not collide

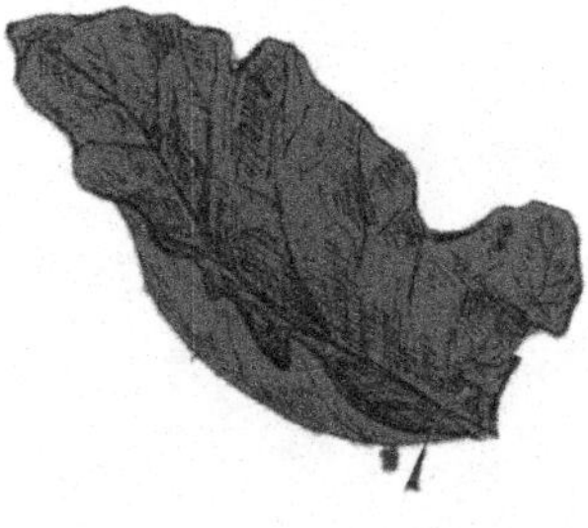

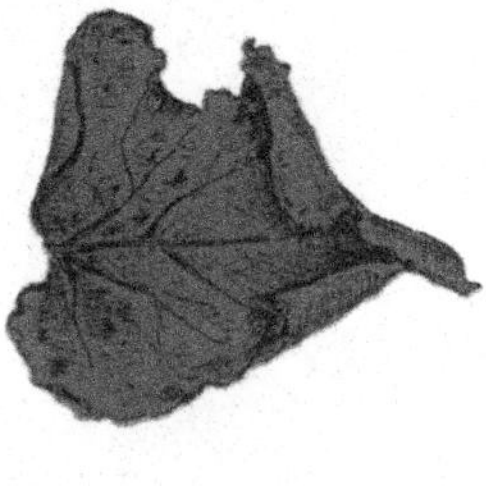